Oliver Twist

Charles Dickens

Adapted by Nigel Flynn

GALLERY BOOKS
An Imprint of W. H. Smith Publishers Inc.
112 Madison Avenue
New York City 10016

This book was devised and produced by
Multimedia Publications (UK) Ltd.

Editor: Nigel Flynn (Acorn Press)
Designer: Janette Place
Production: Arnon Orbach

First published in the United States of America 1985 by
Gallery Books, an imprint of W. H. Smith Publishers Inc.,
112 Madison Avenue, New York, NY 10016

ISBN 0 8317 6596 8

Typeset by Waveney Typesetters, Norwich, Norfolk
Origination by Clifton Studios Ltd., London
Printed in Italy by Amilcare Pizzi SpA., Milan

Contents

The Life of Charles Dickens

Charles John Huffham Dickens was born on 7 February 1812, in the English coastal town of Portsmouth, where his father, John Dickens, was a clerk in the Navy Pay Office. John Dickens was 26 when Charles was born and was an excitable, extravagant man who liked to entertain in style — a style that his meagre salary as a clerk was unable to support. This was to lead him into a succession of financial crises throughout his life.

The second of eight children, Charles was a delicate, sensitive child, unable to join in the play of other children, and he withdrew into books. Later in life, recalling his boyhood days, he wrote: "When I think of it, the picture always arises in my mind of a summer evening, the boys at play in the churchyard and I sitting on my bed, reading as if for life."

The books that he read, introduced to him by his father — books such as *Robinson Crusoe*, *The Arabian Nights*, *Don Quixote* and a child's *Tom Jones* — created for him a world of magic, wonder and adventure, a world that he himself was so vividly to create for others to enjoy in his own books.

At the age of 12 the childhood of Dickens came to a sudden and dramatic end. His father, unable to pay his large debts, was packed off to the Marshalsea Debtors' Prison in London. Within a few days the rest of the family were to join him there — all, that is, except Charles, whose education was cut short and who was made to earn his living, washing bottles, at Warren's Blacking Factory. This experience proved so shocking and humiliating to the boy that it was to haunt him for the rest of his life. "No words can express the secret agony of my soul . . . I felt my early hopes of growing up to be a learned and distinguished man crushed in my breast."

Though soon re-united with his family, the previous easy life enjoyed by Charles was never to return. Two years later, at the age of 14, his irregular and inadequate schooling ended and he began work as a clerk in a lawyer's office in Gray's Inn, London. This experience, again not a happy one, gave him two things — a lifelong loathing of the legal profession and much raw material for many of his later novels.

Dickens then became a reporter on the parliamentary newspaper *True Sun*, where his natural talent for reporting and keen observation was first recognized. He taught himself shorthand and, on the *Mirror of Parliament*, and then the *Morning Chronicle*, he was soon acknowledged as the best parliamentary reporter of the age.

In 1833, now very much the young man about town, Dickens wrote his first piece of fiction: *A Dinner at Poplar Walk*, in the *Old Monthly Magazine*. Asked by the editor to contribute more, under the pen name 'Boz', Dickens wrote a series of pieces that were collected and published in 1836 under the title *Sketches by Boz*.

The modest success of *Sketches* was followed by the enormously popular and successful *Pickwick Papers*, which was published in monthly instalments in 1836 and 1837. Pickwick became a national hero overnight, and his exploits were followed by an average of 40,000 readers. Though not yet 30, Dickens was now rich and famous.

Two days after the publication of Pickwick, Dickens married Catherine Hogarth, daughter of a fellow journalist. "So perfect a creature never breathed," he wrote of her at the time, "she had not a fault." But with time his view of her was to change, and in later years he was to admit, "She is amiable and complying but nothing on earth would make her understand me." They were to separate in 1858, when Dickens was 46.

Throughout his life Dickens enjoyed travelling. In the 1840s he journeyed to Scotland, America, France, Switzerland and Italy. And throughout this period he poured out a succession of novels that exposed the cruelty, hypocrisy and appalling poverty of early Victorian society, novels such as *Oliver Twist*, *Nicholas Nickleby*, *The Old Curiosity Shop*, *Barnaby Rudge*, *A Christmas Carol*, *Martin Chuzzlewit*, and *Dombey and Son*.

Even his novel writing (which continued to be published in monthly instalments) proved inadequate for his boundless energy and restless spirit. In the 1840s, apart from all his major novels, and work on *David Copperfield* (published in 1850), he started a daily newspaper, the *Daily News*, and a weekly magazine, *Household Words*, in addition to writing a travel book *American Notes* and a three-volume *Child's History of England*.

In all that he wrote Dickens strove to draw people together and lead them to a better understanding of each other. As he himself believed, "In this world a great deal of bitterness among us arises from an imperfect understanding of one another."

But as he grew older, the subjects he wrote of grew bleaker and the mood more grim. *Bleak House, Hard Times, Little Dorrit, A Tale of Two Cities, Great Expectations, Our Mutual Friend* and his unfinished novel, *The Mystery of Edwin Drood*, all reflect a growing pessimism.

Despite a steady decline in health, Dickens continued to give dramatic public readings of his works to packed houses in both Britain and the United States, which he visited again in 1867–68. Of these a contemporary witness reported, "He seemed to be physically transformed as he passed from one character to another; he had as many distinct voices as his books had characters; he held at command the fountains of laughter and tears . . . When he sat down it was not mere applause that followed, but a passionate outburst of love for the man."

But the strain proved too much and on 8 June 1870, during a farewell series of talks in England, he suffered a stroke, and the next day he died at his home, Gad's Hill Place, near Rochester, Kent, at the age of 58.

Two days after his death Queen Victoria wrote in her diary, "He is a very great loss. He had a large loving mind and the strongest sympathy with the poorer classes." On 14 June he was buried in Poet's Corner, Westminster Abbey, close to the monuments of Chaucer and Shakespeare.

Charles Dickens in his study at Gad's Hill Place, his home near Rochester, Kent, reproduced by kind permission of the Trustees of the Dickens House (*Dickens' Dream* by R. W. Buss)

Introduction

OLIVER TWIST is one of the most popular stories of all time, and it tells the story of a boy's journey from hell to heaven.

For children like Oliver, England a hundred and fifty years ago was a cruel, hard place. At his birth, Oliver's mother dies. Unloved and uncared for, he grows up in the workhouse, ill-treated and half-starved by the dreadful Mr Bumble, the beadle. When he asks for more food, he speaks for hundreds of thousands of children everywhere whose voices society refuses to hear.

Dickens had a deep desire to expose neglect and abuse and make the world a better place for the poor and weak, and in *Oliver Twist* he uses Mr Bumble and the fiendish Fagin to represent cruelty and tyranny. Fagin is one of Dickens' most evil characters; at one point Dickens refers to him as a "merry old gentleman", a nineteenth-century name for the Devil himself. Be cruel to children, Dickens says, and they will turn to a life of crime: when Oliver arrives in London the Artful Dodger befriends him and takes him straight to Fagin's den.

Oliver is plunged into a nightmare world from which he cannot escape; he tries to, but is hunted down and caught. When his only true friend, Nancy, tries to escape she is horribly murdered.

There are good people in *Oliver Twist* too, including Oliver. In his heart he is not coarsened by the workhouse or corrupted by Fagin. Like Christian in *The Pilgrim's Progress*, he finds peace and safety in the end, helped by Mr Brownlow, Dr Losberne, Rose Maylie and Nancy. In the end goodness wins over evil.

Oliver Twist was Dickens' second novel. After the fun and humour of *The Pickwick Papers*, it rather surprised his readers, but it sold well and added to his growing reputation. Today *Oliver Twist* is the most widely read of all his novels, and Dickens would have been pleased to know that a story which shows "the principle of Good surviving through every adverse circumstance" has remained so popular.

1 In the Workhouse

On a cold, wet night, in a workhouse in a certain town in England, on a day and a date which are unknown, a baby boy was born.

For a long time after he was ushered into this world it remained a matter of doubt whether he would survive. He had no one to help or comfort him but an old pauper nurse and his poor, young mother who lay dying in bed.

Feebly the young woman raised her pale face from the pillow and in a faint voice said, "Let me see my baby before I die."

"Lor bless her heart," said the old nurse. "When you has lived as long as I 'ave and had thirteen children and all on 'em dead 'cept two, and them in the workhouse with me, you'd know better than to take on in that way."

But the young woman just shook her head and stretched out her hand towards the child. She kissed the baby passionately on its forehead with her cold, white lips.

"Keep him safe," she whispered, "and when he's grown up, give him this . . ."

She pressed a gold locket into the old nurse's hand, then gazed wildly round, shuddered, fell back — and died.

"Poor dear," said the old nurse as she stooped to pick the baby up. "It's all over."

By the light of a flickering candle, the old nurse snatched the locket from the dead woman's hand. Opening it, she saw the name 'Agnes' engraved inside.

Then stuffing the locket into her pocket, she carried the crying child out of the room and up a shabby flight of stairs to Mr Bumble's office.

Mr Bumble was the beadle in charge of the workhouse, and on this night — as on most nights — he was entertaining his friends to drinks. They were laughing and joking when the old woman knocked on the door.

"Mr Bumble," she called out, "Mr Bumble!"

"And what do you want?" demanded Mr Bumble rudely as he opened the door.

"It's this baby, begging your pardon, sir."

"Oh, not another one! Well, what is it — boy or girl?"

"Please, sir, it's a boy."

"Name?"

"Sally, sir."

"No, not your name, you fool! The boy's name!"

"Don't know, sir. He 'ain't got no name."

"No name!" boomed Mr Bumble. "Why ever not? What's his mother call him?"

"Mother's dead, sir."

"How very inconsiderate of her! Well, I'll just have to invent a name for him myself."

Mr Bumble went to his desk and took out a notebook. "We name all our fondlins in alphabetical order. The last was an S — Swubble, I name him. So this one must be a T — Twist. Yes, I think I'll call him Twist. Oliver Twist."

"Queer sort of name, if you ask me," replied old Sally.

"Well, nobody did ask you. And you'd better get used to it, Sally. Master Oliver Twist is going to be on our hands for the next ten years!"

Oliver cried lustily. If he could have known that he was an orphan left to the tender mercies of Mr Bumble and the workhouse, perhaps he would have cried even louder.

Nine years passed with little improvement in the condition of the workhouse — or of Mr Bumble's temper. Oliver Twist's ninth birthday found him a pale, thin child somewhat lacking in height. But nature had implanted a good sturdy spirit in Oliver's breast. It had plenty of room to expand, thanks to the spare diet of the workhouse. And perhaps it was surprising that he had survived to celebrate his ninth birthday at all. Be this as it may, however, it *was* his ninth birthday and he was keeping it in the same way as he had all previous birthdays, or for that matter almost every day of his life.

The room in which Oliver and the other boys of the workhouse were fed was a large stone hall with a huge copper pot at one end. Out of this, the master, dressed in cook's uniform, and assisted by one or two women, ladled out gruel at meal-times. Of this delicious concoction each boy had one ladleful, and no more. The bowls never wanted washing. The boys polished them with their spoons till they shone, and when they had performed this operation — which never took very long, the spoons being nearly as large as the bowls — they would sit staring at the large

copper pot with such eager eyes as if they could have devoured it and the very table it was standing on.

For years Oliver Twist and his companions had suffered the tortures of slow starvation. At last they grew so voracious and wild with hunger, that one boy proposed that they should draw lots; whoever drew the shortest should walk up to the master after supper that night and ask for more.

The evening arrived; the boys took their places. The master stationed himself at the copper as usual, his assistants ranged behind him. The gruel was served out and a long grace was said. The gruel disappeared. The boys whispered and nudged each other. Anxiously they drew the lots. And the shortest fell to Oliver!

Young as he was, Oliver was desperate with hunger and reckless with misery. He rose from the table and advancing to the master, basin and spoon in hand, said in a thin, nervous voice, "Please, sir, I want some more."

The master was a red-faced man, but now he turned very pale. He gazed in stupefied astonishment at Oliver for several seconds and then clung to the copper for support.

"What!" he said at length, in a weak voice.

"Please, sir," replied Oliver, "I want some more."

"More! More?" he boomed and he aimed a blow at Oliver's head with the ladle, picked him up roughly by the scruff of his neck, and marched him out of the room shrieking, "Mr Bumble! Mr Bumble!"

The beadle was sitting with his friends when the master burst into his office shouting, "Mr Bumble, begging your pardon, sir, but Oliver Twist has asked for more!"

There was a general start. Horror was

depicted on every face.

"For *more?*" shouted Mr Bumble.

"He did, sir," replied the master.

"That boy will be hung," said a gentleman in a white waistcoat. "I know that boy will be hung."

No one disputed the prophetic gentleman's opinion. An animated discussion took place, and Oliver was ordered into instant confinement. Next morning, Mr Bumble posted a notice on the outside of the workhouse, offering a reward of five pounds to anyone who would take Oliver Twist off the hands of the parish.

"I never was more convinced of anything in my life," said the gentleman in the white waistcoat as he knocked at the gate and read the bill next morning: "I never was more convinced of anything in my life, than I am, that that boy will come to be hung."

2 Apprenticed to a Coffin-Maker

Early that same day Mr Bumble was returning to the workhouse when he encountered, at the gate, Mr Sowerberry the undertaker.

"I have measured up the two women that died last night, Mr Bumble," said the undertaker.

"You'll make your fortune, Mr Sowerberry," said the beadle as he thrust his thumb and forefinger into the coffin-shaped snuff-box offered him by Mr Sowerberry.

"Think so?" said the undertaker. "Well I have you to thank, Mr Bumble, seeing as how you provide me with more business than anyone else in the parish."

"By the bye," said Mr Bumble, "you don't know anybody who wants a boy, do you?" And as he spoke he raised his cane to the poster above him, and gave three distinct taps on the words, 'five pounds reward'.

"Well, I was just thinking, Mr Bumble, I could do with a boy myself. Someone to walk in front of the funeral procession, someone with a pale, sad face, to emphasize the misery, the dismal nature of the occasion."

"That's young Oliver exactly," replied Mr Bumble, grasping the undertaker by the arm and leading him into the building. Within minutes it was arranged that Oliver should go to Mr Sowerberry's that evening.

when Charlotte, the maid, showed Mr Bumble in.

"Mrs Sowerberry! Mrs Sowerberry!" cried the undertaker. "Come here a moment, my dear!"

"Dear me," said Mrs Sowerberry seeing Oliver, who gave a bow, "he's very small."

"He *is* small," replied Mr Bumble, "there's no denying it. But he'll grow, Mrs Sowerberry — he'll grow."

"I dare say he will, Mr Bumble, on our food and our drink. There! Get down stairs, little bag o' bones." And with this, the undertaker's wife opened a side-door and pushed Oliver down a steep flight of stairs to a lonely cell, damp and dark.

"Here, Oliver, you can have some of the cold bits that were put by for the dog. I dare say you ain't too dainty to eat 'em, are you, boy?"

"No indeed, thank you, ma'am," replied Oliver, whose eyes had glistened at the sight of meat and who was trembling with eagerness to devour it.

When Oliver had finished eating his supper, Mrs Sowerberry, taking up a dim and dirty lamp, led the way upstairs.

"You don't mind sleeping among the coffins, do you?" said Mrs Sowerberry. "Not that it

Oliver heard the news in perfect silence. And having had his luggage, which consisted of a small, brown paper parcel, put into his hand, he pulled his cap over his eyes and attaching himself to Mr Bumble's coat-cuff, was led away to a new scene of suffering.

Mr Sowerberry was making some entries into his day-book by the light of a dismal candle

matters whether you do or don't! You can't sleep anywhere else!"

Left to himself, Oliver set the lamp down on a bench and gazed timidly about him with a feeling of awe and dread. Nor were these the only dismal feelings which depressed him. He was alone in a strange place. He had no friends to care for, or to care for him. And he wished, as he crept into his lonely bed that night, that it were *his* coffin; that he could be laid in a calm and lasting sleep in the churchyard, with tall grass waving gently above his head and the sound of church bells soothing him to sleep.

The next morning Oliver was awakened by a loud kicking at the outside of the shop door.

"Open the door, will yer?" cried a voice. "I suppose you're the new boy, ain't yer?" asked the voice again when Oliver had done as he had been told.

"Yes, sir."

"Yer don't know who I am, do yer, Work'us? Well I'm Mister Claypole and you take orders from me, right? Now take down those shutters, yer idle young ruffian!" And with this, Mr Claypole, who in reality was not much older or bigger than Oliver, gave Oliver a hearty kick.

So began for Oliver many months of ill-treatment at the hands of Noah Claypole, who abused him far worse when he learned that Oliver was to lead the funeral procession while he, Noah, was to remain in the shop.

Oliver had been in Mr Sowerberry's employment some three months when an event occurred that was to prove very important in his life.

Seated one dinner-hour in the kitchen, and feeling in a particularly vicious mood, Noah decided to tantalize and aggravate Oliver even more than usual.

" 'Ow's yer mother, Work'us?" he said.

"She's dead, and don't you say anything about her to me!" replied Oliver, a tear rolling down his cheek.

"She was a nice 'un, she was, your mother," continued Noah.

"But yer must know, Work'us, yer mother was a regular bad 'un."

"What did you say?"

"A regular bad 'un, your mother was. Lucky she died when she did, or else she'd be in prison or hung or something."

Crimson with fury, Oliver knocked over the chair and table, seized Noah by the throat, shook him until the teeth chattered in his head

and with one tremendous blow knocked him to the ground.

"Help! Help! Oliver's gone mad!" blubbered Noah. "He'll murder me! Help! Char-lotte!"

Noah's shouts were answered by a loud scream from Charlotte, who rushed into the kitchen, and seizing Oliver began beating him with her fists.

"You mur-de-rous, hor-rid little vil-lain!" she screamed and continued punching the poor child while Noah, who had at last risen from the ground, pommelled him from behind.

The noise and commotion at last roused Mrs Sowerberry who, on entering the kitchen and seeing the proceedings, joined in the fray. When at last they were all three wearied out they dragged Oliver back to the workhouse where Mr Bumble administered yet another thrashing on poor Oliver.

It was not until he was alone in the silence and stillness of his gloomy room, that Oliver gave way to his feelings. When there was no one to see him, he fell down on his knees and, hiding his face in his hands, wept bitterly.

For a long time after his tears had ceased, he remained motionless in this position. Then, looking cautiously round, he quietly crept down the stairs, gently unfastened the front door and peered outside.

The night was cold and dark. Softly, he closed the door and was in the open street. Looking right and left, he followed the road out of town until he came to a footpath leading across some fields. Then, creeping under a hay-rick he lay down and fell fast asleep.

3 Fagin's Gang

The next morning Oliver awoke cold and stiff and so hungry that he was forced to exchange his only penny for a small loaf of bread in the very first village he came to. He had walked no more than twelve miles, when night closed in again. Another night spent in the bleak damp air, made him feel so cold and ill that when he started his journey next morning, he could hardly crawl along.

At last, at the bottom of a steep hill, a stage-coach came along. Desperately, Oliver implored the driver and the outside passengers to stop. But no one took any notice of him. Exhausted as he was, poor Oliver ran alongside the coach a little way before falling, with bleeding feet, on to the rough, wet road. And there he would have remained for ever but for a kindly road-worker who gave him some bread and cheese.

Refreshed, Oliver continued his journey to London. In some villages, large painted signs were fixed up warning all persons who begged that they would be sent to jail. This made Oliver very frightened and glad to be out of them. If he begged at a farmer's house, the dog was set on him, and if he dared show his nose in a shop or at an inn he was threatened with the beadle.

In fact, had it not been for a benevolent old lady who gave him what little she could afford — and more — Oliver's troubles would have most assuredly have ended by his falling dead upon the road.

Early in the seventh morning after he had left Mr Sowerberry's, Oliver limped slowly into the

little town of Barnet on the edge of London. The window-shutters were closed; the street was empty. With bleeding feet and covered in dust, Oliver sat down on a doorstep. After a while the shutters were opened and people began passing to and fro. A few stopped to gaze at Oliver for a moment or two, or turned round to stare at him as they hurried on. But none troubled themselves to ask how he came to be there or to offer him any help. And he had no heart to beg. So he just sat there.

He had been crouching on the step for some time when he noticed the queerest-looking boy he had ever seen staring at him from the opposite side of the street. Though he was a boy of about Oliver's age, he had about him all the airs and manners of a man. Crossing the road, the boy walked up to Oliver and said, " 'Allo, my covey, what's up?"

"I'm very hungry and tired," returned Oliver, tears standing in his eyes as he spoke. "I've walked a very long way. I've been walking for seven days."

"Walkin' fer sivin days! Goin' to London, I 'sp'ose."

"Yes."

"Got any lodgings?"

"No."

"Money?"

"No."

The strange boy whistled. "Well don't fret yer eyelids on that score, young 'un. I know an old gentlemen in London wot'll give you lodgings for nothink."

The offer of shelter was too tempting to resist, especially as it was followed by the suggestion that they eat first. So, with his new friend, who introduced himself as Jack Dawkins, otherwise known as the Artful Dodger, Oliver was taken to a nearby shop and was bought bread and ham and then, at the direction of the Artful Dodger, they proceeded to an inn where a pot of beer was consumed by each.

It was nightfall when they eventually reached the street where the old gentleman lived. And a dirtier or more wretched place Oliver had never

seen. In fact, he was just wondering whether he had not better run away when his companion suddenly said, " 'ere we are, Oliver!" He gave a shrill whistle and thumped on the door three times. "Come on, Fagin, let us in!"

A pair of bespectacled eyes appeared through a grate at the top of the door.

"There's two of you," stated a cold, thin voice. "Who's the other one?"

"A new pal, Oliver Twist."

The heavy old door creaked slowly open. "Fagin, this is 'im. Oliver Twist."

Fagin was an old man with a thick, flowing beard, long grey hair, and a pair of spectacles perched on the end of his nose. Taking Oliver by his cold, limp hand, he said, "Pleased to meet you, Oliver, I'm sure. Very pleased indeed."

Oliver was led up a dark and broken staircase to a small back room. The walls and ceiling were black with age and dirt. The room was hot and

stuffy. A bare table stood in front of a bright fire. Several rough beds were huddled side by side on the floor. Seated round the table were four or five boys, none older than the Dodger.

"Dodger, our friend is hungry. Get him something to eat. Sit down, Oliver. You can watch us play a little game while you eat."

"Thank you, sir."

At this the other boys burst into boisterous laughter, but Oliver sat down as he had been told and ate his supper.

Fagin's little game began at once. First he placed a snuff-box in one pocket of his trousers, then a notebook in the other, and finally a gold watch inside his waistcoat. Then, buttoning up his jacket very tightly round him, he trotted up and down the room waving a stick — like an old gentleman walking about the streets in broad daylight.

Sometimes he stopped at the fireplace and sometimes at the door, pretending to be looking attentively into shop windows. At such times he would suddenly swing round, looking for thieves. Then he would tap all his pockets in turn, to make sure he had not lost anything. And he did it in such a funny and natural way that Oliver laughed until the tears ran down his face.

All this time two boys followed him closely, the Dodger and Charley Bates, getting out of his sight, so nimbly, every time he turned round, that it was impossible to follow their motions. At last the Dodger trod on Fagin's toes, while Charley stumbled up against him from behind; and in that one moment they took from him, with the most extraordinary speed, snuff-box, notebook, pocket-handkerchief, even his old

spectacle-case. If the old gentleman felt a hand in any of his pockets, he cried out where it was and then the game began all over again.

When this game had been played a great many times, Fagin said, "Well done, boys, well done. Enough for one day. I think it's time young Oliver got some sleep!"

It was late the next morning when he woke. There was no one in the room but Fagin. Half asleep, Oliver watched as Fagin took a small box from under the floorboards and placed it carefully on the table. Then, looking anxiously all around, Fagin took out rings, brooches, bracelets and other precious jewels.

Staring round, his eye fell on Oliver's face. The boy's eyes were fixed on him in terror. With a crash, Fagin closed the lid of the box and, laying his hand on a bread knife from the table, he shouted furiously,

"What's this? What do you watch me for? Why are you awake? What have you seen? Speak out, boy! Quick — quick! For your life!"

"I wasn't able to sleep any longer, sir. I'm very sorry if I disturbed you."

"Hmm, did you see any of the pretty things?" asked Fagin, laying his hand on the box.

"Yes, sir."

"Well, now! They — they're mine, Oliver. All mine. Something to live on in my old age. Folks call me a miser. And that's what I am. Only a miser. Now, get up, Oliver, I've a little job for you to do when the Dodger and Charley return."

Later that morning the three boys set out.

They had been walking a long time, when, just as they were emerging from a narrow court not far from Clerkenwell Green, the Dodger suddenly stopped.

"See that old cove at the bookstall?" he asked, pointing to an old gentleman across the road. "He'll do!"

Before Oliver had time to say anything, the Dodger and Charley were across the road and close behind the old gentleman. And to Oliver's utter horror, he saw the Dodger plunge his hand into the old gentleman's pocket, draw out a handkerchief and hand it to Charley.

In an instant the whole business of the handkerchiefs and the watches and the jewels and Fagin's little game became clear. Confused and frightened, Oliver took to his heels. But at that very moment the old gentleman, putting his hand in his pocket and missing his handkerchief, turned round. Seeing Oliver start to run away at such speed, he began shouting, "Stop, thief!" with all his might.

Immediately, a crowd joined in the chase, crying, "Stop, thief! Stop that boy!" Soon their cry was taken up by a hundred voices. After poor Oliver they ran, splashing through the mud and

rattling along the pavements; up went the windows; out ran the people, until, panting with exhaustion, a look of terror in his eyes and perspiration streaming down his face, Oliver was finally felled by a mighty blow.

Jostling and pushing, the crowd gathered round. "Stand aside there! Make way for the gentleman, do!" said the man who knocked Oliver down.

At that moment a police officer made his way through the crowd, and seized Oliver by the collar.

"Is this the boy what robbed you, sir?" asked the police officer.

"I'm afraid it is," replied the old gentleman.

"Afraid! Afraid!" murmured the policeman. "That's a good 'un. Come on, get up!" he said roughly.

"Please, sir, it wasn't me, it was two other boys. They're here somewhere," said Oliver, looking round wildly.

"Come on, you young devil, I've heard that one before. Come on, get up!"

And Oliver, who could hardly stand, was dragged along by his collar at a rapid pace with the gentleman by the officer's side.

"It's Mr Fang the magistrate for you, my lad," said the policeman. "And don't expect any sympathy from him! 'Cos you won't get any."

Indeed he was right. When Mr Fang looked at Oliver when he appeared in court, he gave him an angry scowl. The gentleman bowed respectfully.

"Who are you?" asked Mr Fang, angrily.

"My name, sir," said the man, "is Brownlow."

"Officer! What's this man charged with?"

"He's not charged with anything at all, your worship," replied the officer. "He appears against the boy."

"Appears against the boy, does he?" said Mr Fang, surveying Mr Brownlow contemptuously from head to foot. "Swear him in!"

"Before I am sworn, I must beg . . ."

"Hold your tongue, you insolent, impertinent fellow. How dare you bully a magistrate! I'll have you turned out! Swear this person!" he said turning to the clerk, "I'll not hear another word!"

Reluctantly Mr Brownlow was sworn in.

"Now," said Fang, "what's the charge against the boy? What have you got to say, sir?"

"I was standing at a bookstall . . ." began Mr Brownlow.

"Hold your tongue, sir!" said Mr Fang. "Policeman! Where's that policeman. Now, policeman, what is all this?"

The policeman related how he had taken the charge; how he had searched Oliver and found nothing and that was all he knew.

"Any other witnesses?"

"None, your worship."

"Now, state your complaint against this boy," he said, turning to Mr Brownlow, "or I'll punish you for disrespect to the bench!"

With many interruptions and repeated insults, Mr Brownlow described what he had seen and concluded by saying that he hoped the boy would be dealt with leniently. "He has been hurt already and I really fear that he is very ill."

"Oh, I dare say he is!" replied Mr Fang with a

sneer. "Come now, none of your tricks, you young vagabond. What's your name?"

Oliver tried to reply, but his tongue failed him. He was deadly pale and the whole place seemed to be turning round and round.

"What's your name, you little scoundrel?"

Oliver raised his hand and, looking round, fell heavily to the floor in a faint.

"I knew he was pretending," said Mr Fang. "Let him lie there, he'll soon tire of that."

"How do you propose to deal with the case, sir?" inquired the clerk in a low voice.

"Severely," replied Mr Fang. "He stands committed for three months — hard labour, of course. Clear the court!"

"Stop! Stop! Don't take him away!" cried a man who burst into the courtroom at that very moment, breathless with haste.

"What's this? Who is this person? Clear the court!"

"I saw it all. I keep the bookstall. You must hear me, Mr Fang. I demand to be sworn in!"

"Swear the fellow," growled Fang, reluctantly. "Now, man, what have you to say?"

"I saw three boys: two others and the prisoner, loitering on the opposite side of the street, while this gentleman was reading. But the robbery was committed by another boy. I saw it done."

"You're absolutely certain this is not the culprit?" demanded Mr Fang.

"The boy is innocent!"

"Huh! Pity! Looks like a criminal to me. Case dismissed. Clear the court!"

The court was cleared as directed. Little Oliver Twist was thrown onto the pavement outside. His face was deadly white and a cold trembling convulsed his whole frame.

"Poor boy, poor boy!" said Mr Brownlow, bending over him. "Call a coach, somebody, directly!"

"May I accompany you?" asked the bookstall-keeper.

"Bless me, yes, of course, my dear friend," replied Mr Brownlow. "Jump in. There's no time to lose, poor fellow!"

The bookstall-keeper got into the coach and away they drove.

4 Kidnapped

"Why, how's this?" muttered Fagin, as the Dodger and Charley Bates returned to his house. "Where's Oliver? Where's the boy?"

The two young thieves eyed Fagin sheepishly, but said nothing.

"What's become of the boy?" asked Fagin again, grabbing the Dodger tightly by the collar. "Speak or I'll throttle you!"

"The police got 'im, and that's all about it!" replied the Dodger. "Let me go, will yer?"

And swinging himself free, he picked up a toasting-fork and lunged at Fagin. But with greater agility than one would expect from such a decrepit old man, Fagin skipped back and, seizing up a pot, hurled it at the Dodger.

"Oi, who pitched that 'ere at me?" demanded a deep voice. "Wot's this all about?" The man who growled out these words was stoutly-built with a broad, heavy face and two scowling eyes. Behind him skulked his bull terrier, Bullseye.

"What you up to, Fagin? Ill-treating the boys again, heh? I wonder they don't murder you: I would if I was them!"

"Well, well, Bill Sikes," said Fagin. "You seem out of humour, Bill."

"Perhaps I am," replied Sikes. "I should think *you* was rather out of sorts yourself, throwing pewter pots about the place."

After a while, when all was calm, the Dodger related to Sikes and Fagin the circumstances of Oliver's capture.

"I'm afraid," said Fagin, "that he may say something which will get us into trouble."

"Very likely," returned Sikes with a malicious grin. "You're done for, Fagin!"

"And I'm afraid," added Fagin, looking at Sikes closely, "that if the game was up with me, it might be up with a good many more, and that it would be rather worse for you than it would for me, my dear."

Sikes turned with a fierce look on his face. There was a long pause. "Somebody must find out wot's been done to Oliver," he said finally.

Fagin nodded assent.

"If he hasn't already squealed against us, that is. You must get hold of him, Fagin."

Again Fagin nodded. It was obvious that none of them could go to the police station to find out what had happened to Oliver. But their dilemma was answered by the arrival of Sikes' friend, Nancy.

"Nancy, my dear," said Fagin in a soothing manner, after explaining what he wanted her to do, "What do you say?"

"That it won't do, so it's no use a-trying it on, Fagin."

"She'll go, Fagin, don't you worry," said Sikes. And he was right. After threatening her

with a beating if she refused, Nancy agreed to do as Fagin asked.

So, with a clean apron tied over her dress and her hair tucked up under a straw bonnet, Nancy made her way to the police station.

"Is there a little boy here?" she asked the police officer behind the desk, with a sob. "My poor, dear, sweet little brother! What ever has become of him? Have pity, sir, please. Tell me what's been done to my poor little brother."

"No need to carry on, miss," replied the policeman, kindly. "We haven't got him."

"Haven't got him?" screamed Nancy. "Wherever is he? Oh my poor, dear brother!"

"Why, the gentleman's got him," replied the policeman; and he proceeded to tell Nancy that Oliver had been taken to a house somewhere in Pentonville.

"We must know where he is, my dears," said Fagin when Nancy returned. "He *must* be found. Charley, do nothing till you bring news of him! Nancy, my dear, I must have him found.

I trust to you and the Artful for everything! But wait a moment," he added, unlocking a drawer with shaking hand, "there's money. Don't stop here a minute. Not an instant, my dears! Find him out, that's all! I shall know what to do next, never fear."

And with these words he pushed them from the room and carefully double-locked and barred the door. "He hasn't squealed so far," said Fagin. "If he means to blab among his new friends, we may stop his mouth yet."

Meanwhile, Oliver was recovering in Mr Brownlow's neat house in a shady street near Pentonville. For many days after his arrival, Oliver remained insensible to all the goodness of his new friends. Weak and thin and pallid, he awoke at last from what seemed to have been a long and troubled dream.

"What room is this?" he asked. "Where am I."

"Hush, my dear," replied Mrs Bedwin, Mr Brownlow's housekeeper. "You must be very

quiet, or you will be ill again. Lie down, there's a dear!" With these words the old lady gently placed Oliver's head upon the pillow and smoothed back his hair.

So Oliver kept very still, and soon fell into a gentle doze. He was awakened by the light of a candle. A gentleman with a very large and loud-ticking gold watch in his hand was feeling his pulse and said that Oliver was a great deal better.

Within three days he was able to sit in a chair, well propped up with pillows. Too weak to walk, Mrs Bedwin had him carried downstairs into her own little room, where he was brought some tea by the fireside.

"You're very, very, kind to me, ma'am," said Oliver.

"Well, never you mind that, my dear. Just drink your tea," replied the old lady, sitting down.

Oliver had scarcely finished when there was a soft tap on the door.

"Come in," said Mrs Bedwin, and in walked Mr Brownlow.

"How do you feel, Oliver?"

"Very happy, sir. And very grateful indeed, for your goodness to me."

"Good boy," said Mr Brownlow, stoutly.

"Why! Good heavens! What's this? Bedwin, look there!"

As he spoke, Mr Brownlow pointed to a picture above Oliver's head and then to the boy's face. There was its living copy. The eyes, the head, the mouth; every feature was the same!

Nothing, however, was said to Oliver about the picture. Indeed, on Mr Brownlow's instructions it was removed from the room and stored away.

One evening, about a week after the incident of the picture, as he was sitting talking to Mrs Bedwin, there came a message from Mr Brownlow that if Oliver felt well he should like to see him in his study.

Oliver tapped at the study door. As he entered the room, he saw Mr Brownlow sitting at a table by a window, reading.

"Now," he said in a kind but serious manner. "I want you to pay great attention, my boy, to what I am going to say."

"Oh, don't tell me you are going to send me away, sir! Don't turn me out of doors to wander in the streets. Don't send me back to that wretched place I came from. Have mercy upon a poor boy, sir!"

"My dear child you need not be afraid of my deserting you, unless you give me cause."

"I never will, sir. Never!"

"I hope not. Now, Oliver . . ."

Just then an impatient double-knock was heard at the street door and the servant, running up the stairs, announced Mr Grimwig.

"Hallo! Who's that!" said Mr Grimwig as he entered the study and saw Oliver.

"This is young Oliver Twist, whom we were speaking about," replied Mr Brownlow.

As fate would have it, Mrs Bedwin happened to come it at that moment with a small parcel of books, which a messenger from the bookstall had just delivered.

"Stop the boy, Mrs Bedwin!" said Mr Brownlow. "There's something I want him to take back."

"He's gone, sir."

"Send Oliver with them," suggested Mr Grimwig with a malicious grin, "he'll be sure to deliver them safely, you know."

"What an excellent idea! Oliver, fetch the books for me, would you please?"

Delighted to be of some use, Oliver did as he was asked, and waited cap in hand to hear the message he was to take.

"You are to say," said Mr Brownlow, glancing steadily at Mr Grimwig, "that you have brought the books back and that you have come to pay the five pounds I owe. Is that clear?"

"Yes sir, I won't be ten minutes," replied Oliver eagerly.

"Bless his sweet face." said Mrs Bedwin as soon as Oliver had gone. "I can't bear to let him out of my sight."

"He'll be back in twenty minutes at the latest," said Mr Brownlow.

"You really expect him back, do you?" inquired Mr Grimwig.

"Don't you?" asked Mr Brownlow, smiling.

"No. I do not. The boy has a new suit of clothes on his back, a set of valuable books under his arm and a five-pound note in his pocket. He'll join his old friends the thieves and laugh at you. If ever that boy returns to this house, sir, I'll eat my hat!"

cried Oliver struggling in Sikes' powerful grasp. "Help! Help!"

"I'll soon stop your nonsense, my lad!" exclaimed Bill Sikes. And with these words he tore the books from Oliver's hands and struck him on the head. Then, seizing Oliver by the scruff of his neck, he gave him another blow for good measure. "Come on, you young villain!" he said and dragged the boy into a maze of dark narrow streets and alleys.

"Delighted to see you looking so well, my dear," said Fagin when they arrived. "Why didn't you write and say you were coming? We'd have got something warm for supper."

At this everyone roared with laughter.

"Look at 'is togs, Fagin," shouted Charley Bates, "and 'is books! Wot a gentleman! Oh my eye, what a game!"

"We're delighted to see you looking so well, me dear," said Fagin, bowing in mock humility. "But the Artful had better give you another suit of clothes, for fear you should spoil that nice one."

"They're very pretty," said Charley Bates, picking up the books and pretending to read one of them. "Beautiful writing, isn't it Oliver?" And at this he fell into another bout of boisterous laughter.

"But they belong to the gentleman," said Oliver, wringing his hands. "He'll think I stole them, and so will Mrs Bedwin. All of them who were so kind to me will think I stole them. Have mercy on me and send them back! Please!"

With these words Oliver fell on his knees at Fagin's feet and beat his hands together in

Earlier that same day, in an obscure back room of a public house in the filthiest part of London, Bill Sikes sat brooding over a tankard of ale muttering to Fagin, who sat very ill at ease.

As he spoke, Nancy dressed in bonnet and shawl, burst into the room and said, "The brat's been ill and confined to the house, and . . ."

"After him, Nancy," said Fagin. "He'll have to go out some time. And Bill, you go with Nancy — you may be needed."

Pulling her shawl over her shoulders, Nancy left with Bill Sikes who was followed, at a little distance, by Bullseye.

Meanwhile Oliver, little dreaming that he was within so very short a distance of Fagin, was on his way to the bookstall. He was walking along thinking how happy he was when he was startled by a young woman screaming out very loud, "Oh, me dear brother!" He had hardly looked up when he was stopped by a pair of arms grabbing him tight round the neck.

"I've found him! Oh! Oliver! You naughty boy, to make me suffer such distress . . ."

"Don't," cried Oliver, struggling and kicking. "Let go of me. What are you doing?"

Nancy had caused such a commotion that a small crowd had gathered.

"What's the matter," shouted a woman, "what's going on here?"

"It's me brother Oliver. He ran away from home and almost broke his mother's heart."

"Go home to yer poor mother, you little brute!" shouted Bill Sikes, bursting out of a beer-shop.

"I don't belong to them. I don't know them."

wild desperation.

"You're right, Oliver, you're right. They *will* think you have stolen 'em. Ha! Ha! Ha! it couldn't have happened better!" chuckled Fagin, rubbing his hands.

"Of course it couldn't," replied Sikes. "I know'd that directly I see him coming along with those books under his arm. And them wot kept 'im won't ask no questions arter him for fear they should be obliged to prosecute and so get him hanged. He's safe enough now."

At these words Oliver jumped suddenly to his feet and tore wildly round the room uttering shrieks for help which made the bare old house echo to the roof.

"Wanted to get assistance, call the police, did you?" sneered Fagin, catching Oliver by the arm. "We'll cure you of that, my young friend." And he inflicted a smart blow on Oliver's shoulders with a club that knocked him to the floor. He was just raising it for a second blow when Nancy rushed forward, grabbed it from his hand and flung it into the fire.

"I won't stand by and see it done, Fagin," she cried. "You've got the boy, what more do you want? Let him be — or I'll do something to you that'll bring you to the gallows!"

"Why Nancy!" said Fagin after a pause, during which he and Sikes had stared hard at one another, "You wouldn't do a thing like that, would you? Not to Bill and me surely?"

"Wouldn't I! Take care I don't! You'll be the worse for it Fagin, if I do. So I'm telling you to keep clear of me."

All this time poor Oliver just lay on the floor. Too feeble to resist, he was picked up by Bill Sikes and thrown into another room, where feeling sick and weary, he sank into unconsciousness.

5 The Evidence Destroyed

In the very same town in which Oliver Twist was born, Mr Bumble emerged early one morning from the workhouse-gate and walked with portly carriage and commanding steps up the High Street. He was in the full bloom and pride of beadlehood; and with his head held even higher than usual, Mr Bumble boarded the London coach.

Again and again throughout the journey his eye rested on the following newspaper advertisement

FIVE GUINEAS REWARD

The above reward will be paid to any person who will give information as will lead to the discovery of a young boy named Oliver Twist or throw any light upon his previous history.

Then followed a full description of Oliver's dress, appearance and disappearance, with the name and address of Mr Brownlow.

Arriving in London, Mr Bumble, after consuming a modest dinner of steaks and oysters and ale, proceeded to Mr Brownlow's house in Pentonville.

"Come in, come in," said Mrs Bedwin when Mr Bumble had stated his errand. "I knew we should hear of him. Poor dear! I knew we should. Bless his heart! I said so all along."

Having said this the old lady showed Mr

Bumble into the little back study, where sat Mr Brownlow and his friend Mr Grimwig, who at once burst into the exclamation:

"A beadle! A parish beadle, or I'll eat my hat!"

"I *am* a parish beadle," replied Mr Bumble.

"You come in response to the advertisement?" asked Mr Brownlow, impatiently.

"Yes, sir."

"Do you know where this poor boy is now?"

"No more than nobody," replied Mr Bumble none too helpfully.

"Well, what *do* you know of him? Speak out my friend, if you have anything to say. What do you know of him?"

Mr Bumble put down his hat, unbuttoned his coat, folded his arms and after a few moments reflection, commenced his story.

". . . Therefore, sir, to sum up," said Mr Bumble after having spoken for some twenty minutes, "Oliver Twist is, in my long and bitter experience, treacherous, ungrateful and malicious. He ran away from his master's house after a cowardly and vicious attack on the innocent, helpless lad, Noah Claypole . . . and this after

causing a riot in the workhouse. In short, he's a hardened criminal."

Mr Brownlow paced the room for some minutes, much disturbed by the beadle's tale. At length he ran the bell violently. "I fear it is all too true," he said sorrowfully. "Here is your reward. I would gladly have given you treble if it had been favourable to the boy."

"Mrs Bedwin," he continued when the housekeeper answered his call, "Oliver is an imposter. Never let me hear the boy's name mentioned again. Never!

"He was a dear, grateful, gentle child," retorted Mrs Bedwin, bursting into tears. "I *know* what children are, sir, and have done these forty years."

"You may leave the room, Mrs Bedwin. And remember! I am in earnest."

There were sad hearts at Mr Brownlow's that night after the beadle had left.

On returning home, Mr Bumble walked back up the High Street until he came to a public house. It began to rain heavily at that moment. This determined him. Mr Bumble stepped in and ordering something to drink entered the

parlour, which was deserted save for one solitary customer.

The man who was seated there was tall and dark and wore a large cloak. He had the air of a stranger and by the mud and dust on his coat seemed to have travelled some distance. After having encountered each other's glance several times, the stranger, in a harsh, deep voice, broke the silence.

"I have seen you before, I think," he said. "You are beadle here, are you not?"

"I am the parish beadle, yes," replied Mr Bumble.

The stranger smiled, and nodded his head, as much as to say, he had not mistaken his man.

"Now listen to me," he said, "I came down to this place today to find you out. I want some information from you. I don't ask you to give it for nothing, slight as it is." And as he spoke he pushed two sovereigns across the table.

"Carry your memory back — let me see — some twelve years."

"It's a long time," said Mr Bumble. "Very good. I've done it."

"The scene, the workhouse."

"Good!"

"And the time, night."

"Yes."

"And the place, the lying-in room where a boy was born."

"Many boys," observed Mr Bumble, shaking his head.

"I speak of one: a meek-looking, pale-faced devil who was apprenticed to a coffin-maker and who afterwards ran away to London."

"Why, you mean Oliver Twist!" said Mr Bumble. "I remember him of course. There wasn't a worse . . ."

"It's not of him I want to hear. It's of a woman: the hag that nursed his mother. Where is she?"

"She died last winter. My wife was with her when she died and she could, I believe, throw some light on the subject, should you be interested . . ."

"When?" asked the stranger, hastily.

"Tomorrow," rejoined Mr Bumble.

"At nine in the evening," said the stranger, producing a scrap of paper and writing on it an address. "At nine in the evening, bring her to me there. I needn't tell you to be secret. It's in your own interest."

With these words he led the way to the door, stopping only to pay for what they had drunk. Glancing at the address, Mr Bumble saw that it contained no name. The stranger had not gone far, so he made after him.

"What name am I to ask for?" he said, touching the man on the arm.

"Monks!" answered the man and strode quickly away.

It was a dull, close, overcast summer evening that threatened a violent thunder-storm, when Mr and Mrs Bumble directed their course towards the ruined house erected on a low unwholesome swamp, bordering on the river.

As they stood before this building, the first peal of distant thunder reverberated in the air and the rain poured violently down.

"Hallo there!" cried a voice from above.

Following the sound, Mr Bumble raised his head and saw a man looking out of a door on the second storey.

"Is that the man?" asked Mrs Bumble.

Mr Bumble nodded.

"Then, mind what I told you," she said, "and be careful you say as little as possible, or you'll betray us at once."

"Now," said Monks, when they had all three seated themselves, "the sooner we come to business the better. You were with the hag the night she died and she told you something?" he asked, turning to Mrs Bumble.

"About the mother of the boy you named, yes."

"The first question is, what did she say?"

"That's the second," observed the woman. "The first is, what's it worth?"

"It may be nothing, it may be twenty pounds. Who the devil can say without knowing what you've got to say?"

"Add five pounds to the sum you named. Give me five-and-twenty pounds and I'll tell you all I know."

"Five-and-twenty pounds!" exclaimed Monks.

Reluctantly, he thrust his hand into a side pocket and, producing a canvas bag, counted out twenty-five pounds on the table and pushed

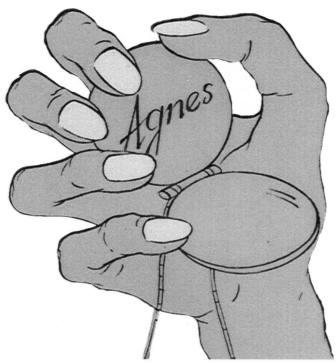

them over to Mrs Bumble. Just then a peal of thunder seemed to shake the whole house. Raising his head, Monks bent forward to listen to what she had to say.

"When this woman, that we called old Sally, died, she and I were alone. She spoke of a young woman who had brought a child into the world some years before. The child was the one you named last night to him," and she nodded towards Mr Bumble. "This young mother, old Sally robbed. She stole from the corpse something the young mother had asked her, with her last breath, to keep for her child."

"She sold it?" cried Monks. "Did she sell it? Where? When? To whom? How long ago?"

"As old Sally told me, with great difficulty, that she had done this, she fell back and died."

"It's a lie!" screamed Monks. "She said more. I'll tear the life out of you both, if you don't tell me!"

"She didn't utter another word," said Mrs Bumble quite unmoved, "but she clutched my gown, violently, with her hand, which was partly closed. And when I saw that she was dead, I removed the hand with force and found that it clasped a scrap of dirty paper."

"Which contained . . .?" asked Monks, stretching forward.

"Nothing. Just a pawnbroker's ticket."

"For what?" demanded Monks.

"There!" replied the woman. And, as if glad to be relieved of it, she threw down a small leather purse, which Monks, pouncing upon, tore open with trembling hands. It contained a little gold locket in which the name 'Agnes' was engraved.

"And this is all?" asked Monks.

"All. Is it what you expected to get from me?"

"It is."

"What do you propose to do with it? Can it be used against me?" demanded Mrs Bumble.

"Never," answered Monks, "nor against me neither. See here! But don't move a step forward!"

With these words, he suddenly wheeled the table aside and, pulling an iron ring in the boarding, threw back a large trap-door, which opened close to Mr Bumble's feet and caused him to retire several paces backwards.

"Look down," said Monks, lowering the lantern. "Don't fear me. I could have let you down, quietly enough, when you were seated over it, if that had been my game."

The two looked down at the turbid water, swollen by the heavy rain, rushing rapidly below. Monks drew the gold locket from his pocket where he had hurriedly placed it, and dropped it into the stream. The three, looking into each other's faces, seemed to breathe more freely.

"Now light your lantern and get away from here, as fast as you can," said Monks. They left in silence. Monks brought up the rear, after pausing to satisfy himself that there were no other sounds to be heard, than the beating of the rain and the rushing of the water.

6 The Burglary

It was about noon the next day when Oliver awoke. The Dodger and Charley Bates had gone out. Oliver was alone in the house with Fagin, who took the opportunity of lecturing the boy on the sin of ingratitude. Smiling hideously, he patted Oliver on the head and said that if he kept himself quiet and applied himself to learning the "business" then he saw no reason why the two of them should not be friends. Then, taking up his hat, he departed, locking the door behind him.

And so Oliver remained all that day, and for the great part of many subsequent days; seeing nobody between early morning and midnight. After the lapse of a week or so, Fagin left the room-door unlocked. From that day Oliver was seldom left alone, but was placed in the constant company of the Dodger and Bates, who for Oliver's benefit, played the old handkerchief game with Fagin.

At other times Fagin would tell them stories of robberies he had committed in his younger days, mixed up with stories so droll and curious that Oliver could not help laughing heartily and showing that he was amused in spite of his better feelings. Thus Fagin prepared Oliver's mind, by solitude and gloom, to prefer any company to that of his own sad thoughts in such a dreary place.

Thus Oliver spent several weeks after his capture. Then, waking one morning, he was surprised to see a new pair of shoes, with strong, thick soles, placed beside his bed. At first he thought that it meant he might be released, a thought soon dispelled by Fagin telling him that he was to take up residence with Bill Sikes, that very evening.

"To . . . to . . . stop there, sir?" asked Oliver.

"No, no, my dear. Not to stop there. We shouldn't like to lose you. Don't be afraid, Oliver, you shall come back to us. Ha! ha! ha!"

Late that afternoon, alone in the house, Oliver heard a knock on the door.

"What's that! Who's there?"

"Me. Only me," replied a voice.

Oliver raised the candle above his head and looked towards the door. It was Nancy.

"Put down the light," said the girl. "It hurts my eyes. I've come from Bill. Come on, you're to go with me."

She took the hand which Oliver instinctively placed in hers, and, blowing out the light, quickly opened the door and passed into the street.

"This way," she said after they had been walking for some time, "in, 'ere." And she pushed Oliver into a dark passageway.

"So you've got the kid," said Sikes, appearing at the top of a steep flight of stairs.

"Yes, here he is," replied Nancy.

"Come here young 'un and let me tell you

something which is well got over at once."

Pulling Oliver into a gloomy room, he snatched his cap off his head and, taking up a pistol, said, "Know wot this is?"

"Yes, please, sir."

"Well then, look here. This is powder; that 'ere's a bullet and this is a little bit of old hat for waddin'."

Carefully, Sikes loaded the pistol. Then he grasped Oliver's wrist tightly and put the barrel so close to his temple that they touched. "If you speak a word when you're out o' doors with me, except when I speak to you, that loading will be in your head without notice. So if you *do* make up your mind to speak without leave, say your prayers first."

For a long time Oliver lay awake that night weary, wretched and afraid, while Nancy sat brooding over the fire and Sikes drank and cursed.

"Now then!" growled Sikes the next morning, "it's half-past five! Look sharp or you'll get no breakfast; its late as it is."

It was a cheerless morning when they got into the street, blowing and raining hard. There were few out of doors in that part of town, for the

"I'm your man as far as I go," he replied.

The night was very dark. A damp mist rose from the river. It was piercing cold too; all was black and gloomy. Oliver sat huddled in a corner of the cart, bewildered with alarm and apprehension. After what seemed to be many miles, the cart stopped. Sikes got out and, taking Oliver by the hand, began walking once again.

They hurried through the main street of a little town, then, quickening their pace, turned up a road and after walking abut a quarter of a mile, stopped before a large, detached house.

"Now," said Sikes, drawing the pistol from his pocket "if you don't do exactly what I say, I'll strew your brains on the grass! Now listen. I'm going to put you through there," and he pointed to a small lattice-window about five feet and a half above the ground. "When you're inside, go along the little hall to the street door, unbolt it and let me in. Right? And remember, no funny business. I'll have you covered.

This was no sooner said than Sikes forced open the window with his crowbar and pushed Oliver inside. In the short time he had had to collect his senses, Oliver decided that he would try to warn the people of the house, even if he were to die in the attempt. With this idea in mind he unbolted the front door, then made towards the stairs.

"Come back!" cried Sikes, "Back! back!"

Scared by the sudden breaking of the dead silence, Oliver tripped and fell. Suddenly, a light appeared and the vision of two terrified

windows were all closely shut and the streets through which they passed, were noiseless and empty.

As they approached the City of London the noise and traffic increased and as they headed south it swelled into a roar of sound and bustle. Sikes, dragging Oliver after him, elbowed his way through the thickest of the crowd.

"Come on, don't lag behind, already, lazy legs. There's miles to go yet."

And so they made their way through and across London with Oliver wondering more and more, as the day progressed, where Sikes was taking him. Kensington, Hammersmith, Chiswick, Kew Bridge, Brentford, were all passed and yet they went on as steadily as if their journey had just begun.

At length they turned into an old public house and ordered some dinner by the kitchen fire. They had some cold meat and, being tired with the walk and getting up so early, Oliver was soon dozing by the fire.

It was quite dark when he was awakened by a push from Sikes.

"Could you give my boy and me a lift?" he heard Sikes ask of a man sitting nearby.

half-dressed men at the top of the stairs swam before his eyes — a flash — a loud noise —smoke — a crash somewhere — and Oliver staggered back.

Sikes grabbed Oliver before the smoke had cleared away. He fired his own pistol after the men, who were already retreating, and dragged the boy out of the house.

"Clasp your arm tighter," said Sikes, then almost immediately, "My God, they've hit him. How the boy bleeds!"

Then came the loud ringing of a bell, mingled with the sound of pistol shots and the shouts of men. Oliver was lifted up and carried out of the house and over the ground at a rapid pace. And then the noises grew confused in the distance and a deadly cold crept over the boy, and he saw or heard no more.

There was little Sikes could see in the mist and darkness, but the loud shouting of men vibrated through the air and the barking of the neighbouring dogs, roused by the alarm bells, resounded in every direction. Sikes again looked round and could now see that the men giving chase were already climbing the gate of the field in which he stood; and that a couple of dogs were some paces in front of them.

Clenching his teeth he threw his cape over the body of Oliver; then, running along a hedge, he dived into the undergrowth and was gone.

The air grew colder as day came slowly on, and the mist rolled along the ground like a dense cloud of smoke. Still Oliver lay motionless and insensible on the spot where Sikes had left him. Morning drew on a pace. The air became sharp and piercing. Rain came down thick and fast, pattering noisily among the leafless bushes. But Oliver felt nothing as it beat against him; for he still lay outstretched, helpless and unconscious on his bed of clay.

At length, he awoke. His left arm hung heavy and useless at his side, his shirt saturated with blood. He was so weak he could scarcely raise himself. He groaned with pain. Every joint in his body trembled from cold and exhaustion. He made an effort to stand up, but shuddering from head to foot, he fell prostrate on the ground.

After a short time he got to his feet again. Staggering like a drunken man, he stumbled on, he knew not where. He looked about and saw at no great distance a house. As he drew nearer, a feeling came over him that he had seen it before. Then, suddenly, he remembered. It was the very same house he and Sikes had attempted to burgle. He pushed against the garden gate, tottered across the lawn, climbed the steps to the front door, then fainted.

Inside the kitchen, the servants heard a noise.

"Open the door," said Mr Giles.

"I will if you come with me," replied Brittles, who after his experience the previous night was still in a nervous state.

No sooner had Brittles opened the door and seen Oliver than he uttered a loud cry.

"A boy!" exclaimed Mr Giles, pushing Brittles into the background. "Why Brittles, look" and with this he seized Oliver by one leg and one arm and lugged him into the hall.

"What is it, Giles?" whispered a soft voice from the top of the stairs. "Hush, or you'll frighten my aunt!"

"It's one of the thieves, Miss Rose, wounded! I shot him, and Brittles held the light."

"Is the poor creature much hurt?" asked Rose as she came quietly down the stairs.

"Wounded desperate, miss. He looks as if he's a-going," replied Giles.

"Poor fellow! He's only a boy. Carry him upstairs, and Giles, treat him kindly, for my sake. Brittles — saddle the pony and go and get Dr Losberne, quick!"

7 A Strange Meeting

At length, and by slow degrees, under the united care of Rose, her aunt, Mrs Maylie, and the kind-hearted Dr Losberne, Oliver recovered from his wound and the fever that had hung about him for many weeks.

As he recovered, Oliver had told them about his life in the workhouse and about Fagin and Bill Sikes and the short period of happiness he had enjoyed at Mr Brownlow's. But it still troubled Oliver that Mr Brownlow and Mrs Bedwin did not know how grateful he had been to them for all their kindness. That they did not know what had happened to him on that fateful day when he had been kidnapped by Nancy and Sikes.

"If they knew how happy I am now, Mrs Maylie, they would be pleased I'm sure," said Oliver one day.

"I'm sure they would," Mrs Maylie replied, "and Dr Losberne has kindly promised that when you are well enough, he will take you to London to see them."

It was not long before Oliver was sufficiently recovered to undergo the journey, and one morning he and Dr Losberne set out in a little carriage belonging to Mrs Maylie. As Oliver knew the name of the street in which Mr Brownlow lived they drove straight there. When the coach finally turned into it, his heart beat so violently that he could scarcely draw his breath.

"Which house is it?" asked Dr Losberne.

"That one — there!" shouted Oliver, pointing to a neat, white house.

The coach rolled on. It stopped. No — that was the wrong house; the next door. It went on a few paces, and stopped again. But alas the house was empty; and there was a notice outside, which read 'To Let'.

Dr Losberne asked the neighbours what had become of Mr Brownlow. He was told that Mr Brownlow had sold off his possessions and left for the West Indies six weeks before with Mrs Bedwin and his friend Mr Grimwig.

The bitter disappointment caused Oliver much sorrow and grief. The idea that they should have gone so far, and carried with them

the belief that he was an imposter and a cheat and that they might think this until their dying day was almost more than he could bear.

Two weeks passed and with it the arrival of warm weather. The Maylie's began preparations for a visit to their country cottage. It was a lovely spot they went to with Oliver, and it was a happy time for the boy who had spent so much of his life in poverty and squalor. The days were peaceful and serene, the nights brought with them neither fear nor care. Every morning Oliver went to a white-headed old gentleman who lived near the little church and who taught him to read better and to write. So three months passed. Spring flew by, and summer came.

Throughout his stay Oliver occupied a little room on the ground floor, at the back of the house. It looked into a garden, beyond which were fine meadows and woods. One beautiful evening, when the first shades of twilight were beginning to settle upon the earth, Oliver sat at his window, reading a book. It had been a sultry day and Oliver, having been very active, sat there in the cool air gradually falling asleep.

He knew perfectly well that he was in his own little room; that his books were lying on the table before him. And yet he was asleep. Suddenly, the scene changed: the air became close and confined, and he thought with a glow of terror that he was in Fagin's house again. Fagin sat in his corner, pointing at him, and whispering to another man who sat beside him.

"Hush, my dear!" he thought he heard Fagin say, "It is he, sure enough. Come away."

"Do you think I wouldn't recognize him?" the

other man seemed to be saying. "If you buried him fifty feet deep and took me across his grave, I should know, if there wasn't a mark above it, that he lay buried there. I should!"

The man seemed to say this with such dreadful hatred that Oliver awoke terrified. But there, there at the window, close in front of him, so close that he could have touched him, with his eyes peering into the room and meeting his: there stood Fagin! And beside him, white with rage or fear or both, were the features of the man he had seen in his "dream".

It was but an instant, a flash before his eyes; then they were gone. But they had recognized him, and he them. He stood transfixed for a moment, and then, leaping from the window into the garden, called loudly for help.

"What direction did they take?" asked Giles.

"Over there," said Oliver, pointing in the direction of the meadows behind the house.

"Come on, Brittles, follow me and keep as close as you can. These men are dangerous."

Oliver followed and in the course of a minute or two Dr Losberne, who had been out walking,

joined them. But their search was in vain. There was not even the traces of recent footsteps to be seen. The four of them stood on the summit of a little hill, commanding a view of the open fields for three or four miles. There was no one.

"It *must* have been a dream, Oliver," said Dr Losberne.

"Oh no, indeed, sir," replied Oliver, "I saw them too plainly for that. I saw them both as plainly as I see you now."

And the earnest look on Oliver's face as he spoke convinced them all of the accuracy of what he said. Still, in no direction was there any sign of the trampling of men in hurried flight.

A further search was made the next day, but with no success. Enquiries were made in the local market town in the hope that someone had seen or heard something of the men, but this effort was equally fruitless, and after a few days the incident was almost forgotten.

Shortly after this the Maylie's went to London to stay for a few days in a quiet but handsome street near Hyde Park, accompanied, as usual, by Dr Losberne and Oliver.

On the second night after their arrival, in another, poorer part of town, Nancy hastily put on her bonnet and shawl, and looking fearfully round, crept quietly out of Bill Sikes' house and made her way to the West End of London.

The clock struck ten. She rushed along the narrow pavement until she reached the hotel where Miss Rose Maylie was staying.

"Now then, young woman," said the man at the door, "and what do you want here?"

"Miss Maylie, please, sir," answered Nancy, desperately. "You must let me speak with her. It's a matter of life or death!" The man, alarmed at the girl's appearance, ran up stairs. Pale and almost breathless, Nancy followed and entered the room. Seeing a slim and beautiful girl, she said, "I'm about to put my life and the lives of others in your hands. I am the girl that dragged little Oliver back to old Fagin's on the night he went out from the house in Pentonville."

"You!" said Rose Maylie.

"I, lady! But I have stolen away from those who would surely murder me if they knew I had been here, to tell you what I have overheard. Do you know of a man called Monks?"

"No," replied Rose.

"He knows you and knows you are here, for it was by hearing him tell the name of the place that I found you out."

"I never heard the name," said Rose, "who is he?"

"Well, some time ago and soon after Oliver was put into your house on the night of the robbery, I — suspecting this man Monks — listened to a conversation held between him and Fagin in the dark. I found out from what I heard that Monks had seen Oliver with two of our boys on the day we first lost him and recognized him as the same child that he was watching for, though I couldn't make out why. A bargain was struck with Fagin, that if he got Oliver back he should give him a certain sum of money, and he was to have more money for making him a thief which this Monks wanted for some purposes of his own."

"But for what purpose?" asked Rose.

"I don't know. I was afraid they might see me, so I left and didn't hear any more. And I saw him no more until tonight."

"And what happened then?"

"The first words I heard Monks say were these: 'So the only proof of the boy's identity lies at the bottom of the river and the old hag that got them from the boy's mother is rotting in her coffin.' They laughed and then Monks says that though he had got the young devil's money now, he'd rather see Oliver hauled before some court and imprisoned for some capital crime!"

"What is all this?" asked Rose.

"The truth, lady. 'In short, Fagin,' says he, 'you never laid such snares as I'll do for my young brother, Oliver'."

"His brother?" exclaimed Rose.

"Those were his very words," said Nancy. "Now it's growing late and I have to reach home without suspicion of having been here. I must get back quickly."

"This man Monks must be investigated," said Rose. "Where can I find you again when necessary?"

"Every Sunday night from eleven until the clock strikes twelve, I will walk on London Bridge — if I am alive."

Sobbing loudly, the unhappy Nancy turned away; while Rose, overpowered by the extraordinary interview, sank into a chair and tried to make some sense of what Nancy had said. Disturbed by these revelations, Rose passed a sleepless night. And with the new day, she was still in a quandary about what to do when Oliver came bursting into the room: "I have seen the gentleman, Mr Brownlow, who was so good to me!"

"Where?" asked Rose.

"Getting out of a coach and going into a house," replied Oliver. "I didn't speak to him — I couldn't speak to him, for he didn't see me. But Giles asked for me whether he lived there, and the servant said he did. Look here, here's the address," and he opened a scrap of paper.

"Quick," said Rose, "tell them to fetch a coach immediately and Oliver, be ready to go with me. I'll take you there directly."

In little more than five minutes they were on their way. And when they arrived, Rose left Oliver in the coach and saw Mr Brownlow privately.

"I shall surprise you very much, I have no doubt," she said to Mr Brownlow and another gentleman who was introduced to her as Mr Grimwig. "But you once showed great goodness to a very dear young friend, Oliver Twist, and I am sure you will take an interest in hearing of him again."

No sooner had the words escaped her lips than Mr Grimwig banged his fist on the table and growled, "A bad one! I knew that boy would come to no good. I'll eat my hat if he's not a bad one!"

"Do not heed my friend, Miss Maylie, he does not mean what he says. Now, tell me what you know of this poor child."

Rose at once, in a few simple words, told all that had befallen Oliver since he left Mr Brownlow's house, reserving only Nancy's information for Mr Brownlow's ear alone.

"Thank God the boy's safe and well!" said Mr Brownlow. "This is great happiness to me, great happiness. But where is he? Where is Oliver?"

"He's waiting in the coach outside."

"At this door?" Without another word, he hurried out of the room, down the stairs and into the coach.

"Send Mrs Bedwin here!" said Mr Brownlow, ringing his own front door bell.

"My dear old nurse!" cried Oliver.

"God be good to me!" cried the old lady. "It's my innocent boy! I knew he'd come back. How well he looks, how like a gentleman's son . . ."

Leaving Oliver and Mrs Bedwin to compare notes, Mr Brownlow led Rose into another room and there heard a full account of her interview with Nancy. Rose then explained that she had told no one else of what Nancy had said, not even Dr Losberne, for fear that he would not keep it a secret.

"We must meet Nancy on London Bridge as arranged," said Mr Brownlow, "and find out more about this Monks. Monks is the key to this mystery. Monks is behind everything!"

8 Fatal Consequences

On the very same night that Nancy, having lulled Bill Sikes to sleep, hurried to see Rose Maylie, there advanced towards London, by the Great North Road, two persons well acquainted with Oliver's history.

They toiled along the dusty road until they passed through Highgate, when the man stopped and called impatiently to his female companion,

"Come on, can't yer? What a lazy bones yer are, Charlotte."

"Is it much farther?" asked the girl, almost breathless with fatigue.

"Much farther! Yer as good as there," said Noah Claypole. "Look there! Those are the lights of London."

Through these streets Noah Claypole walked, dragging Charlotte after him. At length he stopped in front of a public house, dirtier and shabbier than any he had yet seen.

"The Three Cripples," he said, looking up at the sign. "Now then, keep close at my heels and come along!"

Charlotte obediently followed and together they entered the dingy house.

"We want to sleep here, tonight," said Noah, "and while you're at it give us some cold meat and a drop of beer, will yer?"

The two were ushered into a small back bar and refreshment brought to them. The landlord then went off to prepare their room and was just returning when Fagin, in the course of his evening's business, entered.

"Hush!" said the landlord, "there's strangers in the other room. They're robbers from the country."

Fagin heard this with great interest. Mounting a stool he looked through a small pane of glass into the bar where the two sat eating. "Yes," he whispered, "I like that fellow's looks.

He'll be one of us; he knows how to train the girl already. Don't make as much noise as a mouse, my dear, and let me hear 'em talk."

Fagin again applied his eye to the glass, and turning his ear to the partition, listened attentively.

"No more jolly old coffins, Charlotte," he heard Noah say, "but a gentleman's life for me my girl. And if yer like yer shall be a lady."

"I should like that well enough, dear," replied Charlotte, "but it won't always be as easy as it was robbing old Sowerberry's till."

"Tills be blowed! There's more things besides tills to be emptied. There's pockets, houses, mail-coaches, banks . . ."

He stopped suddenly as the door into the small bar opened and in walked Fagin.

"A pleasant night, sir, but cool for the time of year," he said, rubbing his hands. "From the country, I see, sir?"

" 'Ow d'you know that?" replied Noah.

"We have not so much dust as that in London," replied Fagin, pointing from Noah's shoes to those of his companion, and from them to two bundles.

"Yer a sharp feller," said Noah.

"Why, one needs to be sharp in this town, and that's the truth." And he beckoned the landlord to bring more drinks.

"Good stuff that," observed Mr Claypole, smacking his lips.

"My dear!" said Fagin, " 'A man needs to be always emptying a till, or a pocket, or a house, or a mail-coach, or a bank, if he drinks it regularly'."

No sooner had Noah heard his own words than he fell back in his chair, pale and terrified. "Don't mind me," said Fagin. "It was lucky it was only me that heard you. It was very lucky it was only me."

"I didn't take it," stammered Noah, "it was all her doing! It was Charlotte what done it."

"No matter who did it, my dear!" replied Fagin, "I'm in that way myself, and I like you for it."

"In what way?" asked Noah, innocently.

"In that way of business," rejoined Fagin, "and so are the people of the house. There's not a safer place in all this town for people like us, than The Three Cripples. And I'll tell you more. I have a friend who can gratify your wish and put you in the right way of business."

"I wouldn't mind something very light," admitted Noah. "Just to tide me over."

"A little fancy work, perhaps? Something in the spying line? My friend wants somebody who would do a piece of work well — and keep quiet about it — very much."

"Why, now you mention it, I shouldn't mind turning my hand to something, sometime. Something in the sneaking way, where it was pretty sure work and not much more risk than being at home."

"Good," said Fagin, leaning over the table,

after Charlotte had taken the bundle up stairs, "I want you to do a piece of work that needs great care and caution."

"Well, don't yer go shoving me into danger. That don't suit, that don't, not one little bit, I tell yer!"

"There's not the slightest danger in it — not the very smallest. I want you to follow a woman and tell me where she goes, who she sees, and, if possible, what she says — and to bring me back all the information as quickly as you can."

"An old woman?"

"A young one."

"Who is she?"

"One of us. She has found out some new friends, my dear, and I must know who they are."

"I was a regular cunning sneak when I was at school, Fagin, I'm yer man."

"I knew you would be," cried Fagin, elated by the success of his proposal.

"Where is she? Where am I to wait for her? When am I to go?"

"All that, you shall hear from me at the proper time my dear. You keep ready and leave the rest to me."

That night and the next and the next again, Noah Claypole sat ready to turn out at a word from Fagin. Six nights passed, six long weary nights, and on each Fagin came with a disappointed face and said that it was not yet time. On the seventh, a Sunday, he returned and said,

"She goes out tonight. Come with me, quick!"

They left the house stealthily and hurrying through a labyrinth of streets arrived at length before a public house. They entered and Fagin held Noah by his coat behind a curtain. He pointed to a young woman who was looking down sadly at the table.

"Is that her?" asked Noah.

"Yes," said Fagin. "Wait until she turns her face so you can see her plainly."

At that moment, Nancy obligingly turned round.

"I see her now," said Noah, "I should know her among a thousand."

Nancy soon got up and left. Noah exchanged a look with Fagin and darted out. By the light of the street lamp he saw the girl's retreating figure, already at some distance before him. He advanced as near as he dared and kept on the opposite side of the street. Nancy looked

nervously round. She seemed to gather courage as she advanced and began to walk with a firmer step. The spy kept his distance, but never once took his eye off her.

The church clocks chimed three quarters past eleven as two figures emerged on London Bridge. It was a very dark night. A mist hung low over the river. At nearly the centre of the bridge, Nancy stopped. Noah stopped too, and shrinking into one of the recesses which surmount the piers of the bridge, he watched and waited.

The hour had not struck two minutes when a young lady, accompanied by a gentleman, walked up to Nancy.

"Not here," she said hurriedly. "I'm afraid to speak to you here. Down the steps, yonder."

Quickly, Noah went to the spot Nancy had

pointed to and hid.

"Put Monks into my hands," Noah heard the gentleman say, "and leave him to me to deal with."

Noah then heard Nancy tell Mr Brownlow what Monks looked like and where he would find him. "He's tall and strongly made, but not stout. His face is dark, like his hair and eyes. I've only seen him twice and both times he was covered up in a large cloak, but on his throat, when he turns his face, there's . . ."

"A broad red mark, like a burn."

"You know him?" exclaimed Nancy.

"I think I do," said Mr Brownlow. "We shall see. It may not be the same. Now, you have given us the most valuable assistance. What can I do to help you?"

"Nothing, sir," answered the girl, weeping. "You can do nothing to help me. I am past all hope."

"Don't speak thus," pleaded Rose. "There must be something we can do."

"No, nothing! God bless you. Goodnight, goodnight! You must go before someone sees us!"

Mr Brownlow drew his arm through Rose's and gently led her away. As they disappeared Nancy sank to the pavement and sobbed bitter tears. After a while she rose and with feeble and tottering steps climbed the stone stairs to the street above.

Noah remained motionless for some minutes after Nancy had gone, then, peeping out to make sure nobody was about, darted away at his

utmost speed to Fagin's house.

"At last! At last!" muttered Fagin when the boy returned. No sooner had Noah told Fagin what he had seen and heard than a bell rang gently. Fagin crept to the door and presently returned with Bill Sikes.

"Tell me again — once again, just for him to hear," said Fagin, pointing to Sikes as he spoke.

"Tell me what?" asked Sikes.

"About Nancy!" said Fagin, clutching Sikes by the wrist. "You followed her?" he said to Noah.

"Yes."

"To London Bridge?"

"Yes."

"Where she met two people?"

"So she did."

"A gentlemen and a lady who asked her to give up all her pals and to describe Monks, which she did, and to tell which house it was that we meet at and go to, which she did, and what time the people went there, which she did. She did all this. She told it all every word without a threat,

50

did she not?" screamed Fagin, half mad with fury.

"All right," replied Noah. "That's just what she did!"

"Hell's fire!" cried Sikes, breaking free from Fagin's grip. "Let me go!"

Flinging the old man from him, he rushed from the room.

"Bill, Bill!" cried Fagin. "You won't be too — violent, Bill? Not too violent, Bill, for safety."

Sikes made no reply but, pulling open the door, dashed into the street. Without a pause, without once turning his head, his teeth set tightly, the robber did not relax a muscle until he reached his own door. He opened it softly with a key, strode lightly upstairs and entering his own room, double locked the door and lifting a heavy table against it, drew back the curtain of the bed.

"Get up!" he yelled.

"Bill," replied Nancy. "Why do you look like that at me!"

The robber placed his heavy hand on her mouth.

"Bill, Bill, I — I — won't scream or cry —hear me — tell me what I've done!"

"You know, you she-devil! You were watched tonight. Every word you said was heard."

"Spare my life, for the love of Heaven," cried Nancy, clinging to him in despair.

Sikes struggled, violently, to release his arms.

Freeing one arm, he grasped his pistol and with all his force beat it twice upon the upturned face that almost touched his own. Nancy staggered and fell, nearly blinded with the blood that rained down from a deep gash in her head. Sikes, staggering backward to the wall, seized a heavy club and struck her down with one swift blow.

9 The Pursuit

Twilight was beginning to close in when Mr Brownlow alighted from the hackney-carriage outside his house and knocked softly at the front door. The door being opened, a sturdy man got out of the coach and positioned himself on one side of the steps, while another man, who had been sitting on the box, dismounted too. At a sign from Mr Brownlow, they helped out a third man, and taking him between them, hurried him into the house. This man was Monks.

They walked up the stairs without speaking, with Mr Brownlow leading the way into a back room. "If he gives you any trouble," he said to the two men holding Monks, "drag him into the street and call for the police."

"How dare you kidnap me and bring me here by force!" shouted Monks.

"As I said a moment ago," replied Mr Brownlow, "you are free to go. But if you do I will call the police immediately, and prefer my charges publicly."

Plainly disconcerted, Monks hesitated.

"It is because I was your father's oldest friend," said Mr Brownlow, "that I am moved to treat you gently. I know that your name is not Monks — it is Edward Leeford. I knew your father well and was engaged to marry his sister who died many years ago on the very day we were to be married."

"This is all mighty fine," said Monks, "but what do you want with me?"

"I also know that you have a brother," said Mr Brownlow, "a brother whose name when I spoke it earlier startled you."

"I have no brother. You know I was an only child. Why do you talk to me of a brother?"

"The only child of your father's *first* marriage, it is true," said Mr Brownlow. "But after your parents separated, your father met and fell in love with a beautiful young girl called Agnes Fleming, who died giving birth to their child in a workhouse. Your father, as you know, had already died while on business in Rome.

"Later, many years later, it chanced that a poor boy fell into my care, a boy whom I recognized because of the likeness he bore to a portrait of Agnes your father had left in my care before he went abroad. That boy, as you know, is Oliver Twist."

"I never heard the name before," cried Monks, looking more and more nervous at Mr Brownlow's revelations.

"And I also know that you planned to ensnare Oliver into a life of crime and have him murdered so that you could have all your father's money — money that was left to both you and Oliver."

"You — you — can't prove anything against me," stammered Monks.

"We shall see," returned Mr Brownlow, cooly. "When I lost Oliver I knew that you alone could solve the mystery and as I had heard that you were in the West Indies, I made the voyage. There I learned of your life of crime and that you had left months before for London. And I have

searched to find you ever since. But not until Nancy told me where you might be found did I have a clue as to your whereabouts."

"And now you do see me," said Monks boldly, "what are you going to do about it? You can prove nothing. You can't even prove that Oliver was the son of my father and this Agnes."

"You know as well as I do that you destroyed the only piece of evidence when you threw the locket bearing her name into the river. Nancy heard you tell Fagin that. Nancy is now dead, brutally murdered, the newspaper says."

"I — I — know nothing of that . . ."

"Then sign this confession stating what I know to be true, or I will hand you over to the police for robbery and fraud."

Monks paced up and down, meditating with dark and evil looks on his prospects of evading Mr Brownlow's choice, when Mr Grimwig burst into the room to say that Sikes had been cornered down by the river.

"Go and see what happens, Grimwig, and make sure that they take Fagin too. Now, have

you made up your mind?" he asked, turning to Monks.

"Yes," replied Monks. "If you agree not to tell the police and let me go, I'll sign the confession."

By the time Mr Grimwig reached the house on the river where Sikes was believed to be hiding, a small crowd had gathered. Some shouted to those who were nearest to set the house on fire, others roared to the police to shoot Sikes dead on sight. There was another roar when the door to the house was at last forced open.

Panic-stricken by the violence of the crowd, and the sound of approaching footsteps, Sikes climbed out on to the roof-top, carrying a rope, with which to lower himself to the ground.

"They have him now," cried a man from the crowd. There was another roar.

Sikes set his foot against the stack of chimneys, fastened one end of the rope tightly and firmly round it, and with the other made a strong running noose. At the very instant he brought the loop over his head, before slipping it under his arm-pits, Mr Grimwig saw him and shouted. As if struck by lightning, Sikes suddenly staggered, lost his balance and tumbled over the parapet. The noose was at his neck. With an unearthly screech of terror he plummeted towards the ground. There was a sudden jerk, a convulsion of the limbs and the murderer swung lifeless against the wall.

At two o'clock the following afternoon Fagin was arrested by the police, acting on information given to them by Mr Brownlow. In due course he was tried and sentenced to death. As they brought him from the condemned cell to the gallows he struggled desperately for an instant, then sent up cry upon cry that penetrated even those massive walls.

A great multitude had already assembled as the day dawned. The windows were filled with people, smoking and playing cards to pass the time. The crowd were pushing, quarreling and joking. Everything told of life and animation but one dark cluster of objects in the very centre of all — the black stage, the gallows, the rope and the hideous apparatus of death.

Epilogue

So the fortunes of those who have figured in this tale are nearly closed. With his portion of his father's will Edward Leeford, still calling himself Monks, fled to America, where after a long confinement for fraud, he died in prison.

Noah Claypole was given a free pardon after having testified againt Fagin and found his true vocation as a government informer.

Mr and Mrs Bumble, after having confessed to Mr Brownlow of their part in hiding Oliver's true identity, were deprived of their jobs and reduced to great misery, finally became paupers themselves in that very same workhouse in which they had once inflicted such suffering on so many others.

The Artful Dodger, finally caught in the act of picking a pocket, impressed all at his trial by his arrogance and cleverness: as a result he was given a lengthy prison sentence with which Fagin would have been well pleased.

And as for Oliver, he was adopted by Mr Brownlow and with Mrs Bedwin went to live in the country close to the house where Rose and Mrs Maylie lived. And there they were visited a great many times in the course of the year by Mr Grimwig, whose odd and eccentric manner did not mellow with the years. Thus joined together a little society, whose condition approached as nearly to one of perfect happiness as can ever be known in this changing world.